The Wonderful World of Disney

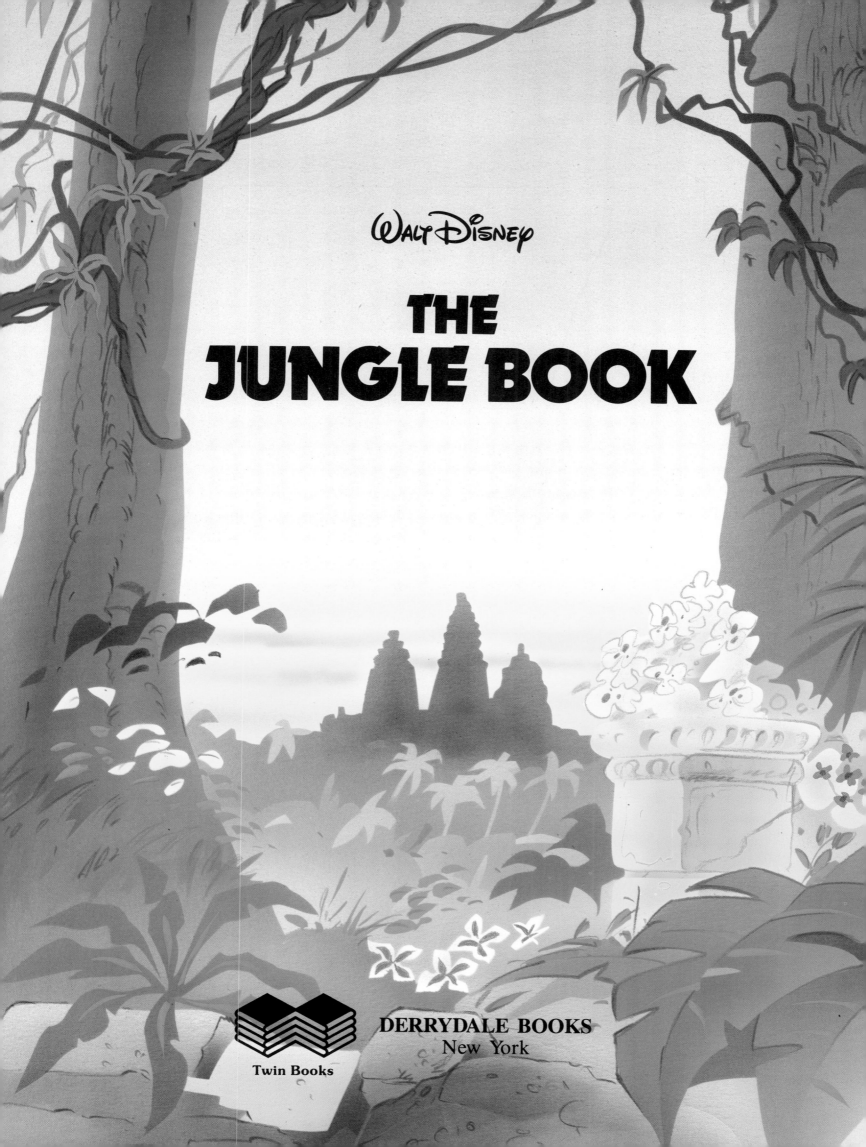

Walt Disney

THE JUNGLE BOOK

DERRYDALE BOOKS
New York

Twin Books

One day, deep in the jungle, Bagheera the black panther heard a strange noise. It sounded like a Man cub, crying. He followed the sound until he came to a river.

In the tall grass on the river's edge, Bagheera found a broken boat.

In the boat was a
basket, and in the basket
was the Man cub, who
seemed to be abandoned.
Bagheera wondered what
to do with the little
creature, who must have
been hungry because he
cried very loudly.

Then the panther remembered a wolf family that he knew, and he thought that perhaps the mother wolf wouldn't mind caring for one more cub. He took the basket in his mouth and carried it through the jungle.

Bagheera came to the wolf den, where
he left the basket and crept into the
bushes to watch.

The mother wolf and her cubs gathered around the basket. They sniffed at the little stranger. "What kind of a cub is this?" asked the mother wolf. The Man cub stopped crying and smiled at her. "We'll call you Mowgli," she said to the baby, "and we will be your new family."

The mother wolf cared for Mowgli, and the wolf cubs played with him. Mowgli was happy to live with the wolf family. As the years passed and Mowgli grew, he learned to walk, to scratch like a wolf, and to play wolf games with his adopted brothers and sisters.

On Mowgli's tenth birthday, Bagheera came to visit. He told the wolves that Shere Khan, the man-eating tiger, was planning to kill Mowgli.

Mowgli hugged his old friend Bagheera. "I'll be all right," he said. "No old tiger can scare me." Mowgli growled to show Bagheera how fierce he could be.

That night Bagheera met with the wolves to discuss the problem. "I think Mowgli must leave at once," he said. "He isn't safe here anymore. I will take him to the Man village." The wolves were very sad to let Mowgli go away because they loved him dearly, but they had to agree that it was the only wise thing to do.

There was no time to waste. Bagheera took Mowgli with him into the jungle the very next day, despite the boy's protests. Mowgli was very quiet, thinking about his wolf family. They traveled far, and that night Bagheera and Mowgli climbed a big tree to sleep.

Just as Mowgli dozed off, Kaa, the
snake, found the sleeping boy. The crafty
snake spoke soothingly, and soon had
Mowgli under his spell.

Kaa hypnotized Mowgli with his stare as he wrapped his long tail around the helpless boy. "What a good supper you will make," he hissed.

Kaa opened his big jaws to devour Mowgli.

Just then Bagheera awoke. With a glance he saw what was happening.

The panther spun around
in a flash and attacked
Kaa with his sharp claws.
The snake let go of his
prey and fell to the ground.
"Are you all right?"
asked Bagheera. Mowgli
nodded, and Bagheera
patted his head. "You are
not safe in the jungle
anymore, my friend," he said.

17

The following morning
Mowgli awoke to the sound
of marching. He climbed
down from the tree, leaving
Bagheera asleep. A line of
elephants filed past,
trumpeting a military march.

At the end of the line came a very small elephant. "Hello!" said Mowgli. "Would you like to join our troop?" asked the little elephant.

Mowgli practiced marching like an elephant, while Hathi, the big elephant general, shouted commands to his troop.

When Mowgli and the little elephant bumped into each other, the whole line of elephants collided.

Hathi trumpeted another command and all the elephants lined up at attention, with the small elephant and Mowgli at the end. Hathi inspected each elephant in turn. When Hathi saw the boy at the end of the line, he lifted him up with his trunk.

"Who are you and what are you doing?" he demanded.

"I'm Mowgli," answered the boy defiantly. "And I'm practicing to be a soldier."

Just then Bagheera arrived and explained the situation to Hathi.

Bagheera and Mowgli continued on their journey. "You're lucky I saved you from Hathi," scolded Bagheera.

Mowgli glared at him. "I was having fun," he said stubbornly. "I can take care of myself."

"That's what you think," snorted Bagheera, "but there's a lot you don't know. The jungle can be a dangerous place."

As soon as Bagheera turned his back,
Mowgli dashed away through the jungle.
"That old panther is boring," he muttered.
"And I'm not going to the Man village."
Just then he heard singing.

Mowgli came to a clearing where a big bear was happily singing to himself.

"I can take care of myself," said Mowgli. "Bagheera doesn't think so, but it's true."

The bear thought for a moment. "You must be Mowgli," he said. "I've heard about you. Well, little fella, if you were a bear you'd have nothing to worry about."

"Teach me to be a bear," said Mowgli.
Baloo put Mowgli on his lap, and began to explain how to be a bear.

"First you've got to learn how to roar like this," said Baloo, letting out an ear-splitting roar. Mowgli practiced roaring, then boxing with Baloo.

"And then, of course, you've got to know how to eat," said Baloo, with a twinkle in his eye. He broke into a merry song, which he and Mowgli sang as they danced and picked fruit off the trees.

Mowgli and Baloo went off together without a thought about Bagheera, who was very worried. When Mowgli found a flock of vultures, he showed them his dance, and they joined in.

But the fierce tiger, Shere Khan, had finally found his prey. He leaped out of the bushes and swatted the vultures away. They flew off into the thunderstorm.

"At last I've got you," growled Shere Khan with a smile.

"I'm not one bit afraid of you!" said Mowgli, even though the tiger made him very nervous.

"There's hardly any sport in this," yawned Shere Khan. "Perhaps I'll count to ten so you can run. It'll make it more interesting." With that the tiger began to count.

The vultures had flown into a nearby
tree, and now they shouted to Mowgli to
run. But Mowgli grabbed a stick and
prepared to fight as Baloo had taught him.

Shere Khan finished his counting, and opened his eyes. When he saw Mowgli standing fearlessly before him, he gave a ferocious roar and leaped for the kill.

But the tiger was stopped in midair, because Baloo had arrived just in time, and was hanging onto Shere Khan's tail with all his might.

"Run, Mowgli!" Baloo shouted, and Mowgli ran.

Shere Khan chased after the boy, but with Baloo holding his tail he couldn't run fast.

A vulture swooped down and grabbed Mowgli, carrying him to safety. But the boy could hear Shere Khan attacking Baloo. "Let me down!" shouted Mowgli.
A mighty lightning crack was heard, and a nearby tree burst into flames.

Mowgli snatched up a burning branch. "I'm coming, Baloo!" he shouted bravely, holding the burning branch in the air.

He sneaked up behind Shere Khan and tied the torch to the tiger's tail. Fire was the king of the jungle's only fear, and he raced away in a panic.

Baloo and Mowgli hugged each other in relief. "You saved my life," they said to each other at the same time.

Just then Bagheera appeared. He was happy to see Mowgli, and Baloo told him what had happened. The three friends decided to rest for the night before continuing their journey.

While Mowgli slept, Baloo covered him with leaves to keep him warm. "I'm going to miss you, little fellow," he whispered.

The three traveled all the next
morning, until they reached a clearing.
"See, there!" said Bagheera.
"The Man village!" said Mowgli, pointing.

They looked at the Man village down in the valley. They were quiet as they thought about Mowgli's departure. They could hear someone singing a sweet song.

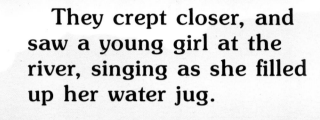

They crept closer, and
saw a young girl at the
river, singing as she filled
up her water jug.

Suddenly Mowgli thought the village
might not be such a bad place after all.

"Go ahead!" prompted Bagheera, from the bushes. Mowgli offered to carry the water jug for the girl.

"Come back to visit," added Baloo, as Mowgli and the girl walked away.

"My name is Mowgli," the boy said.
The girl smiled at him.

Mowgli looked back to wink at his friends, but they had already turned back to the jungle. "I think Mowgli will like the Man village," said Bagheera.

"Yes," agreed Baloo. "But he would've made a great bear anyway." The two friends hummed as they walked along, knowing that the little Man cub would be happy and safe.

This 1988 edition published by Derrydale Books, distributed by Crown Publishers, Inc., 225 Park Avenue South New York, New York 10003

Directed by HELENA Productions Ltd. Image adaptation by Van Gool-Lefevre-Loiseaux

Produced by Twin Books 15 Sherwood Place Greenwich, CT 06830

Printed and bound in Hong Kong

ISBN 0-517-67006-2

h g f e d c b a

The Wonderful World of Disney